# TWISTER'S
# BIG BREAK

Based on the TV series *Nickelodeon Rocket Power*™
created by Klasky Csupo, Inc. as seen on Nickelodeon®

SIMON SPOTLIGHT
An imprint of Simon & Schuster Children's Publishing Division
1230 Avenue of the Americas, New York, New York 10020

Manufactured in the United States of America

First Edition
4 6 8 10 9 7 5

ISBN 0-689-84748-3

Library of Congress Catalog Card Number: 2001095196

# TWISTER'S BIG BREAK

### by Adam Beechen

### illustrated by Fran Talbot and Juliet Newmarch

## Simon Spotlight/Nickelodeon

New York　　　London　　　Toronto　　　Sydney　　　Singapore

# chapter 1

Twister Rodriguez sat at a table in the Shore Shack and twisted a paper napkin into shreds. Then he took another napkin and started twisting all over again.

"Dude!" his best friend, Otto Rocket, exclaimed. "Go easy on the napkins! They don't grow on trees!"

"Actually," their pal Sam Dullard said, "the paper in the napkins does come from trees."

"I can't help it," Twister told them. He looked around the restaurant and saw that nearly all the tables were filled with kids from Ocean Shores.

In the crowd he saw Eddie, Prince of the Netherworld, sitting with Oliver Van Rossum. Trish and Sherry were hanging out in a corner booth. Twister's normally obnoxious older brother, Lars, was here with his buddies, Pi and Sputz. Even Otto's neighbors Mr. and Mrs. Stimpleton were here, although Mr. Stimpleton didn't look happy about it.

Twister felt the butterflies in his stomach do a loop-de-loop. "You guys know how nervous I get whenever I show one of my extreme-sports movies for the first time!"

Otto's older sister, Reggie, patted Twister on the back. "No sweat, Twister, you're an awesome director," she assured him. "All of your movies totally rock! I'm sure this one will too."

"How can it not?" Otto wondered aloud. "I'm the star!" Twister's movies usually put Otto and his incredible stunts in the spotlight.

Sam could see their friend was still nervous. "You just need some premovie munchies," he told Twister. "Nothing calms the nerves like nachos!"

At that moment, in fact, Reggie's and Otto's dad, Ray, came out of the kitchen with a bowl of nachos he and his friend Tito Makani had whipped up. He was walking to Twister's table when a slick young man in a suit waved him over.

Ray looked the man up and down. "Is it already time for my annual checkup from the health inspector?"

"I'm not the health inspector," the man assured him. "I was just wondering if I could get a double decaf mocha latte."

"You probably could," Ray nodded. "But not here. However, I can make you a gut-buster milk shake, right after the big premiere!"

The man looked around. "Premiere? Of what?"

"Only the latest extreme-sports extravaganza from Mr. Twister Rodriguez! Have a seat," Ray said, walking away with the nachos. The man looked interested and took a chair.

Ray put the plate on Twister's table. "You're on, Twist!"

Twister gulped as Ray walked over to the TV in the middle of the restaurant and rested his finger on the VCR's START button. Tito moved to the light switch.

Twister stood up and looked out at the humongous crowd. "Hey, everyone," he said nervously. "Thanks for coming. I hope

you like my latest movie. It stars Otto Rocket."

Otto stood up and took a bow as everyone applauded. Reggie rolled her eyes and dragged her brother back into his chair.

"And it's called, *Dare to Grab Some Air*," Twister added.

The lights went out and the tape started. Twister sat back down and nervously reached for another napkin.

# chapter 2

Everyone in the Shore Shack oohed and aahed as Otto soared through ollies and nollies, 360s and 540s, catching seriously sick air on the vert ramps at Madtown Skate Park and grinding stylishly down curbsides.

Otto did stunts no one had ever seen before, because he had a way of just making things up. And Twister had a way of making everything Otto did look great on camera.

Twister's movie moved as fast as lightning, from one stunt to the next, catching Otto from all angles, to the tunes of the fast, rocking music Twister had chosen.

When the movie ended, everyone in the Shore Shack was out of breath! No one had seen a movie like it. Even Twister's earlier movies seemed slow in comparison. When Ray turned the lights back on, the people in the Shore Shack didn't just sit there and clap, they stood and cheered.

"Right on, Twister," they yelled.

"Twis-ter! Twis-ter," others chanted.

Reggie urged him, "Take a bow, Twister."

Twister grinned from ear to ear, stood up, waved to everyone, and took a deep bow. He was a hit! He couldn't stop smiling as a crowd formed around him.

"Excellent use of depth of field,

Twister," Oliver told him. "Impressive."

"Truly a work of dark genius," Eddie agreed.

"It was all right," Lars admitted, "but next time you should make a movie of me whompin' you!"

"Yeah," said his mush-mouthed pal Sputz. "Thadded beeyafunneemoovee!"

"Ooh, Twister, we're so proud of you," Mrs. Stimpleton squealed, pinching Twister's cheek. She turned to her husband. "Aren't we, Mervy?"

Mr. Stimpleton held the plate of french fries he was finishing. "It wasn't too terrible," he grumbled. Then he leaned in closer to Twister and whispered, "But I mostly came for the french fries! They beat the pants off some of the concoctions Violet makes me eat!"

As the audience filed out of the Shore Shack, Twister's friends surrounded him.

"See?" Reggie said, high-fiving him. "I knew it'd be a smash!"

"Yeah, Twist, that was kickin'," Otto agreed, sharing a knuckle-punch finger-wiggle with his pal. "Of course, how could you go wrong with such a talented cast?"

"Excuse me," said an unfamiliar voice. "Can I talk to you for a minute, Twister?"

Reggie, Otto, and Sam moved aside, and the slick young man in the suit walked up to Twister. "My name is Tad Tadsworth, and I thought your movie was absolutely supremo. Really tip-top."

"Uh, thanks," Twister replied, puzzled. "Glad you liked it."

Tad put his arm around Twister's shoulder. "Twister, I work in advertising for Speed Demon Super Scooters, and while watching your movie, I had a first-rate campaign-concept spark: What if our next sizzle piece was filmed by someone dead center in our target market?"

Twister scratched his head. "Huh?"

Tad smiled. "I want you to make a short movie just like this one that I can show to my bosses. Only, instead of a skateboard, the stunts will all be done on our scooters! If what you come up with is half as good as what I saw here tonight, you could be headed for stardom. First the advertising industry, then Hollywood!"

"Excellent!" Sam exclaimed.

"Right on," Reggie and Otto said at the same time.

Twister's eyes grew as big as gut-buster milk shake glasses. "Whoa," he said, grinning again. "This could be my big break!" Then his grin faded. "But I guess I'll have to ask my parents."

"Absolutely," Tad replied, nodding. "That's very smart of you. Real brainpower, Twister. You ask them, and when they say yes, call me and we'll get started."

He handed Twister a glossy business card, shook his hand, and walked out.

Twister couldn't stop smiling. "Whoa," he said again.

# chapter 3

In the Rockets' garage Reggie was printing out a new article for her 'zine, while Otto oiled the wheels on his skateboard.

Across the room Sam was stuffing extra padding into his helmet when Twister bounded in, looking as happy as he did the night before at the premiere. "Guess what?" he said. "My parents said I could make the ad movie for Speed Demon Super Scooters!"

Reggie, Otto, and Sam rushed over to him. "Excellent," they said, breaking into a little dance.

"Go, Twister! Go, Twister! It's your birthday, it's your birthday," they chanted together.

Twister smiled. "So I called Mr. Tadsworth and asked him to send three scooters over!"

At that very moment a truck screeched to a stop in front of the Rocket house, and a burly deliveryman carried three boxes up to the garage. "Delivery for Maurice Rodriguez," he said.

"Over here," Twister said, sheepishly raising his hand at the mention of his real name. The deliveryman dropped the boxes and walked back to his truck.

Twister looked down at the boxes. "Man," he said, as though he didn't believe it, "I'm really gonna make a movie for this company, and if they like it, I'll get to make more, and then I'll make movies for movie theaters! I'll be a totally famous director—like I always wanted to be—if I make this a rockin' scooter movie!"

Suddenly he looked up at his friends, panicked. "What if I beef it? What if the ad movie totally bites? What if I leave the lens cap on?"

"Whoa, Twist, stress less," Otto urged, clapping his pal on the shoulder.

"He's right, Twister," Sam agreed. "If you worry about beefing, chances are you will. Take it from an expert at worrying!"

"You know you won't be making it alone, Twister," Reggie assured him. "We'll help you!"

"Really?" Twister said, looking at them gratefully.

"Sure," Reggie answered, walking him over to her computer. "I'll make a bunch of

posters asking kids who want to be extras to come down to Madtown for the filming!"

"I'll cook up a bunch of slammin' scooter stunts," Otto said with a grin.

Sam reached for one of the boxes and started opening it. "And I'll take one of these scooters apart and see just what it can—and can't—do!"

Twister looked around at his friends. "You guys totally rule," he said.

chapter 4

Over the next few days Sam examined each and every piece of the Speed Demon Super Scooter, analyzing them with his computer to learn just how fast the sleek silver scooter could go.

Otto took another of the scooters out to the homemade half-pipe in the Rocket backyard, where he experimented with hundreds of new stunts. He wrote down the ones he liked.

And Reggie used her in-line skates to race all over Ocean Shores, tacking up posters asking for extras for Twister's movie.

While his friends rehearsed the stunts they planned over and over, Twister prowled around Madtown with his camera, thinking of angles and shots he could use for the movie. Every time he started getting nervous about filming day, he reminded himself how much his friends were helping him, and the nervousness turned into excitement.

🚀 🚀 🚀

Finally it was time to film. Dozens of kids, having seen Reggie's posters, were waiting excitedly around the park when Twister, Reggie, Otto, and Sam showed up with the Speed Demon Super Scooters.

Oliver, Eddie, Lars, Pi, Sputz, Trish, Sherry, and a ton of other kids and adults milled about. Madtown's owner, Conroy

Blanc, who was also a teacher at the kids' school, twisted one of his long dreadlocks between his fingers. "Man," he said, "I haven't seen this many people at the park since Free Snow Cone Day!"

One of the adult extras in the movie tapped Conroy on the shoulder. "Is it safe to let these kids do all these stunts?" he wanted to know.

"Hey, I wouldn't tell any beginning riders to try these stunts at home by themselves," Conroy answered. "But these kids are expert riders who've been doing it for a long time. Plus they've practiced and practiced, and they're wearing all the right protective gear. And I'm trained to help if anything goes wrong."

Elsewhere Twister felt himself getting nervous again. "I've never made a movie in front of this many people before!"

"Just do what you do best," Reggie told

him, "and everything will be cool."

Twister nodded, taking a deep breath. "All right," he said finally. "Let's make a movie!"

🚀 🚀 🚀

Twister pointed the camera at Otto as he raced the scooter down the side of Madtown's vert ramp, then up the other side and high into the air, where he held on to the handles as the scooter spun beneath him.

When Otto started dropping toward the ramp again, he got the scooter underneath him and landed smoothly, speeding toward the flat bottom of the ramp.

Twister swung the camera to the crowd, who cheered madly. "Speed Demon, Speed Demon, Speed Demon," they chanted, led by Trish and Sherry.

Later Twister caught all the action as Reggie, Sam, and Otto staged a scooter sprint down Madtown's curvy racecourse. The kids weaved in and out of one another's paths, trading the lead, as the crowd clapped and urged them on.

The kids crossed the finish line at the same time, passing Eddie, who was waving a checkered flag. He turned to the camera as the racers went by and shouted, "Dude, that's fast!"

Next Twister turned in place with his camera as Reggie raced her scooter in fast, tight circles around him. When she finally came to a stop, Twister wobbled, dizzy. "Are you okay?" Reggie asked, concerned.

"Are you kidding?" Twister answered, giddy. "That shot was wicked!"

After filming a short segment where Sam showed beginners how to start riding a scooter, Twister set up Otto's greatest stunt: Otto was going to leap with the scooter off a short ramp and over five trash cans!

"Are you sure Otto can do this?" Sam asked Reggie nervously.

"It's a long jump," Reggie admitted. "But if anyone can do it, the Otto-man can!"

"I just hope he doesn't trash my trash cans," muttered Conroy, who'd been closely monitoring the action.

Twister stationed himself at the base of the ramp, so his camera would catch Otto as he flew over. On top of the ramp Otto tightened his chin strap, stretched, and focused. Twister took another deep breath, trying not to be nervous. "Action!" he yelled.

Otto started down the ramp, going faster and faster on the scooter, then leaped over Twister and his camera into the sky! He flew over the first can, then the second, then the third.

The crowd went completely silent as the scooter dropped toward the ground—and

cleared the last trash can by just a few inches.

The crowd went wild! Filming was over, and it had gone perfectly.

Twister high-fived all of his friends who had teamed up to pull him through. "That's a wrap," he cried happily.

# chapter 5

Twister, Otto, Sam, and Reggie stood in a conference room in the offices of Speed Demon Super Scooters, at the far end of a long conference table. Tad Tadsworth and three other executives wearing clothes as fancy as Tad's sat at the other end. Behind them was a large TV.

"Twister," Tad said, beaming as he leaned forward, "we are just so psyched to see your movie. I've told everyone here all

about you, and we really feel like this campaign will be the one to put our scooters over the top!"

"We know you've got a fresh eye," said one of the other executives.

"A fire in your belly," another agreed.

"Your finger on the pulse of what's groovy, hip, and young," said the third, nodding.

Twister wasn't sure what they were talking about—it sounded almost like another language. He cleared his throat and took a sip from a glass of water given to him by Tad's assistant. "Well, I worked really hard on it, but I couldn't have made this movie without my friends Otto, Reggie, and Sam," he said, gesturing to his pals.

"Right, right," Tad replied, in that tone of voice people use when they aren't really listening. "Arnold, Wedgie, and Pam. Pleased to meet you. Come on, Twister, show us your stuff. Let's see some movie magic!"

Reggie leaned over to Sam. "Did he just call me 'Wedgie'? "

"How do you think I feel?" Sam replied. "I mean, do I even look like a 'Pam'? "

Twister put the videotape into the VCR and turned on the TV. "Here it is," he said. "I call it, *Speed Demons and Rocket Riders*." He nodded to one of the men who had moved over to the light switch, and the room went dark.

Twister crossed his fingers and sat back down as the tape started to play.

Five minutes later, when the tape was done and the lights came back on, Twister looked first at his friends, who smiled and nodded encouragingly, and then at Tad and his friends at the end of the table. They all appeared very serious, with their hands folded in front of them.

Tad looked at the executives, who looked back at him. Tad nodded. Then he faced Twister and leaned forward.

"We love it," Tad shouted, breaking into a huge grin. "Twister, it's genius! Exactly what we were hoping for!"

"The film reaches out, grabs you, and gives you a vigorous shake," said one of the executives.

"Home run city," another said approvingly. "Out of the park!"

"The movie makes our scooters look like the three P.H.'s," said the last executive. "Phresh, Phat, and Phantastic!"

Reggie rolled her eyes. "Could you be more out-of-date?" she muttered.

"So, what happens next?" Twister wanted to know. He'd never been so happy before. "Do I get to make another movie?"

"Well, next we have to show this to our

bosses," Tad told him. "But trust us, they're gonna fall right out of their loafers for it!"

Otto leaned forward. "What do we do?"

Tad smiled. "You run along home with Twister, and we'll call you when our bosses give us the thumbs-up, which I'm sure will be soon!"

Tad came around the table and stuck out his hand to Twister. "Twister, believe me when I say this is going to be big, very big!"

"Cool," Twister said.

Tad opened the door for all of them. "Bye now, Twister and friends. Talk to you soon!"

The kids stepped out into the hall, and the conference room door closed behind them.

## chapter 6

"I don't like that Tad-Tad guy," Reggie said as they walked away from the door. "Our names aren't that hard to remember."

"What's important is he liked the movie," Twister reminded her. "He said it was genius!"

"Still, I don't trust him," Reggie said firmly.

"This is only the beginning," Twister thought aloud dreamily. "I can see it now, my name up in lights! I'm gonna make a million movies, and they're gonna be like Mr. Tadsworth said: Big . . . very big!"

They reached the desk of Tad's assistant. Twister put his empty glass back on her desk. "Thanks for the water," he said.

The assistant's intercom beeped, and the kids heard Tad's voice: "Miranda, could you come in here? We're ready to order lunch."

"Right away, Mr. Tadsworth." The assistant stood up and smiled at the kids. "You can find the elevators, right?" She hurried away toward the conference room.

The kids turned to leave just as the intercom crackled. The assistant hadn't turned it off.

"Tad," they heard one of the men say, "that kid's movie is brilliant! You're not really going to let him take the credit for it, are you?"

They heard Tad laugh. "Are you crazy? I'd never let anyone other than myself take credit for something that brilliant! Tomorrow at nine A.M., I'm telling the big bosses that I made that film—then they'll have to promote me to senior vice president!"

"What about the kid?" another man wanted to know.

"What about him?" Tad replied. "He didn't sign any contract, and we've got the tape right here. By the time it comes out, there'll be nothing that kid can do about it! And if it comes down to his word against mine, who's going to believe some little surf rat?" All the executives laughed at this.

Twister went pale and his grin vanished. "I don't believe it," he whispered.

"Those jerks," Otto said, gritting his teeth.

"They-they're lying, cheating . . . liars,"

Sam stammered. He looked like he was about to cry.

"I knew I didn't trust him," Reggie said, shaking her head.

"This was going to be my big break," Twister said sadly. "Now it's down the tubes!"

# chapter 7

The four friends sat around a table at the Shore Shack an hour later. None of them could believe what they had heard in the Speed Demon Super Scooters' offices. "What Mr. Tadsworth's doing is wrong," Reggie said firmly to Twister. "He's taking advantage of you just because you've never done anything like this before."

"That movie is yours," Sam agreed. "He's stealing!"

"There's no way I want to be the star of a stolen movie," Otto said. "That creepo doesn't deserve to have my best moves on his tape!"

"But you heard him," Twister reminded them. "I didn't sign a contract. There's nothing that says that tape is mine."

"There's nothing that says it's his either," Reggie pointed out. "If we stole it back from him, it'd be yours again, and there's nothing he could do about it!"

"But is it right to steal something, even if it's something that's been stolen from you?" Twister wondered.

Tito came over, carrying a tray of extra-large sodas, which he placed in front of them. "Your food will be coming in a minute," he told them. "I'm trying something new—sweet and sour fries!"

"Hey, let's ask Tito about our problem," Otto suggested.

Twister told Tito everything they'd been through with Tad. "Tito, is it wrong to take the tape back?" he asked anxiously.

Tito leaned back in his chair and scratched his chin. "The Ancient Hawaiians had a saying: 'A cup of water taken from the ocean still belongs to the ocean. And what is taken from the ocean must always be returned to the ocean.'"

Twister threw his hands up in the air. "Why didn't the Ancient Hawaiians ever make any sense?"

"I think I understand," Reggie said. "You're agreeing with us, right? Twister should get the tape back."

"But how do we get into those offices, get the tape before Tad shows it at nine tomorrow morning, and get out again?" Sam wanted to know.

Tito smiled. "The Ancient Hawaiians had another saying," he said. "'A king can

be mistaken for a hula girl if he's wearing a grass skirt.'"

Twister rolled his eyes again. "Kings in skirts? What were the Ancient Hawaiians talking about?"

Tito put an arm around Twister's shoulder. "They're saying a good disguise can be a good plan." He smiled, and the kids leaned forward. "Now, here's *our* plan . . ."

# chapter 8

The next morning just before nine, Reggie, Otto, Sam, Twister, and Tito stood outside the Speed Demon offices. Reggie and Otto stood on two of the scooters Tad had sent them. Twister stepped back and looked at Tito. "Tito, man, I don't think I've ever seen you in a coat and tie!"

Tito set down his briefcase to tug at his tight collar. "I'm used to wearing swimsuits, little Twister cuz," he admitted, "but sometimes other suits come in handy!"

He turned to the rest of the kids. "Everyone know the plan?" Otto, Reggie, and Sam nodded. "Then we'll see you in a couple of minutes."

Tito and Twister walked into the building, leaving their friends behind on the sidewalk.

🚀 🚀 🚀

The elevator doors opened, and Tito and Twister walked into the offices. They passed desks and cubicles until they reached the desk belonging to Miranda, Tad's assistant. "Hi, I'm Twister Rodriguez, here to see Tad Tadsworth," Twister said.

"I'm sorry," Miranda replied, "Mr. Tadsworth is going into a meeting and can't see you now."

Tito leaned down to look her in the eye. "Please tell Mr. Tadsworth that Mr.

Rodriguez's attorney is here too."

Miranda gulped. Just then Tad came around the corner to stand in front of them, and Twister saw he was carrying the tape! "Miranda, have you seen—" he started to say, then he saw Twister and Tito.

"Hello, Twister," he said suspiciously. "Who's your friend?"

Tito stuck out his hand. "I'm the famous island attorney, Howie Wannasooya," he said. "We're here for that tape you're holding."

Tad looked scared for a second, then he recovered. "This tape is something I filmed myself," he said.

"You're lying," Twister replied. "I made that movie and you know it!"

Tad looked at Tito and smiled, shrugging. "Kids. Aren't they cute?"

"Mr. Tadsworth, I have reason to believe you're not being truthful," Tito said. "I'm sure you remember the important case, Makani vs. Stimpleton, in which the courts ruled that . . ." Twister was amazed at how much like a lawyer Tito really sounded!

Tad rolled his eyes and pointed down the hall. "Sorry, but I'm late for a meeting."

Tito raised his voice so everyone in the office turned to listen. "Mr. Tadsworth, I came a long way to talk to you for five minutes!"

With everyone looking at him, there was no way Tad could duck out. "Sorry, sorry," he said, trying to get Tito to quiet down.

"As I was saying," Tito started again, "the courts ruled for Makani, who really was a nice island bruddah . . . uh, I mean . . ."

🚀 🚀 🚀

The elevator doors opened again, and Reggie, Otto, and Sam peeked out. Down the corridor, they saw Tito and Twister

distracting Tad, just as they had planned it. Otto looked at Reggie. "Ready?" he asked.

She nodded, buckling her chin strap. Sam held the elevator's DOOR OPEN button.

"Let's roll," Otto said, and he and Reggie pushed their scooters into the corridor. They moved so fast on the scooters that they came up behind Tito and Twister before anyone in the office even saw them.

Otto, in the lead, sped past Tito and ripped the tape out of Tad's hands! Quickly he turned left down a row of cubicles, while Reggie peeled off in the other direction.

Tad dashed after Otto. "Come back here with that tape!"

After making Twister's movie Otto knew everything about the scooter and made amazing twists and turns to keep ahead of Tad. "If I don't have that tape for my meeting, I'll be fired," Tad yelled.

"Too bad, so sad," Otto yelled back.

Suddenly one of the guys who'd been in the conference room with Tad jumped in front of Otto! Otto stopped quickly and saw Reggie cutting across the corridor behind the man. Otto quickly tossed the tape under the man's arm to his sister. "Peel out, Reg," he yelled to her.

Reggie caught the tape and turned her scooter back toward Tito and Twister. Tad and the man from the conference room were catching up to her.

"Help," she cried as she passed Tito and Twister. Twister, thinking quickly, pulled open Tito's briefcase. Papers flew everywhere, blinding the men so they slipped and fell all over each other.

"Hurry up, guys," Sam yelled from the elevator, "before they catch up to you!"

Tito, Twister, and Otto raced to follow

Reggie to the elevator. Sam held the doors open for them as they packed inside.

"Close the doors, Squid," Twister shouted as Tad and the other man came running up.

As the doors started closing, Tad screamed, "Give me that tape, or I'm ruined!"

"See ya," Twister answered, "wouldn't wanna be ya!"

The doors closed in Tad's face.

# chapter 9

That night a crowd had gathered in the Shore Shack for another of Twister's movies. Twister stood up in front of all of his friends and cleared his throat. He wasn't nervous this time—he *knew* this movie rocked.

"I learned a lot from making this movie," he began. "But mostly I learned who my real friends are—they're the people who look out for you and help you when you get into trouble. Thanks, Reg, Otto, and Sam." Twister's three friends smiled as everyone clapped.

Twister then pointed to Tito, who was sitting at a table in the back. "And a mega thank-you to Tito Makani!"

Everyone clapped again. "You the man, Tito," Otto shouted above the noise.

"And thanks to everyone for coming," Twister finished. "You're a better audience than four jerks in suits any day!"

With that the lights went out and the tape started to play. The title came up on the screen: *Speed Demons and Rocket Racers*, followed by, "Directed by Twister Rodriguez." Everyone cheered again, this time for Twister. He smiled.

🛼 🛼 🛼

After the movie Twister accepted congratulations from everyone. They all told him it was his best movie yet. Twister didn't say it, but he agreed with them.

"So long, Eddie," Twister said to the last kid out, leaving just himself, Otto, Reggie, Sam, Ray, and Tito in the Shore Shack. Twister was about to sit down when someone came into the restaurant—Tad. And he didn't look happy.

"It took me all day to explain to my bosses about the tape," he growled. "But they won't fire me if I bring it back to the office. So I'm only going to ask once: Give me back that tape."

The kids smiled at one another. "No problem, Mr. Tadsworth," Sam said cheerfully. Twister and his pals had known Tad was going to show up sooner or later, and they were ready for him.

Sam ducked behind the lunch counter and pulled out a tray holding stacks and stacks of videotapes. "We spent all day making lots and lots of copies, so I'm sure we can spare one for you!" he said.

Tad looked at all of the tapes. "You . . . you made copies?"

"Uh-huh," Twister said. "We sent them all over the place too! I guess maybe you won't be the one to give me my big break. We even sent one to a lawyer—a *real* lawyer."

Hearing this, Tad noticed Tito for the first time standing there, wearing his usual Hawaiian shirt, sandals, and shorts. Tito waved politely at Tad. "How's it going, sneaky business cuz?"

"Oh," said Ray, as though he remembered something. "We also sent one to the Better Business Bureau and told them all about what happened. You'll probably hear from them tomorrow."

"Oh, no," Tad moaned, grabbing his head. "Now I *really* am ruined!"

"Cheer up, Tad," Twister said kindly.

"Maybe a gut-buster milk shake would make you feel better."

Tad thought about it, then nodded. "Maybe you're right. Can I have one, please?"

"You probably can," Twister answered, "but not here! We reserve the right not to serve lying, cheating, creepy jerks! Hit the road!"

Ray, Tito, and Twister's friends high-fived Twister as Tad slunk out of the Shore Shack. "Excellent burn, Twist-a-mundo," Otto told him. "What are you gonna do for an encore?"

"I've already got an idea for a new movie," Twister told them. "It's about four kids who smash the plans of an evil mastermind!"

"Sounds like something I'd go see," Reggie said with a smile. "What are you gonna call it?"

Twister grinned. "How about, *Rocket Raiders of the Stolen Tape?*"

They all high-fived him again, agreeing that it was a perfect title.

## About the Author

**Adam Beechen** has written scripts for episodes of the Nickelodeon TV series *Rocket Power*, *The Wild Thornberrys*, and *Rugrats*. He is also the author of several books featuring *Rocket Power* and *The Wild Thornberrys*. He lives in Los Angeles.

Adam considers having been given the chance to write shows and books for such great characters as Otto, Reggie, Sam, and Twister to be his "big break!"